ART

Written and illustrated by Bob Reese

CHILDRENS PRESS®

CHICAGO

Thanks to my wife, Nancy, for her ideas and help in writing "School Days." A special thanks also to Fran Dyra for her inspiration and editing.

Library of Congress Cataloging-in-Publication Data

Reese, Bob.
    Art / written and illustrated by Bob Reese.
      p.   cm. — (School days)
    Summary: A teacher shows her class various kinds of
art activities that they can do.
    ISBN 0-516-05578-X
    [1. Schools—Fiction. 2. Art—Fiction. 3. Stories in
rhyme.] I. Title. II. Series: Reese, Bob. School days.
PZ8.1.R255Ar   1992
[E]—dc20   92-12187
                                   CIP
                                   AC

WELCOME TO
MISS NATALIE'S
CLASS-ROOM 21

Today I want
to teach you art.

Art is fun.
How do we start?

We can use scissors and glue.

We can use painting, too.

We can tie a rope.

We can carve some soap.

We can draw a toy.

We can draw a boy.

Let's paint a picture

of what we like.

A flower, some fruit,

a boat, or a bike.

Let's see.

Pretty!

Some mice, that's nice.

You kids are smart.
You do great art.

Teacher, paint what you like today!

Well, I like to paint
a pretty place . . .

so, I will paint . . .

my face.

WORD LIST

a	fun	paint	teacher
and	glue	painting	that's
are	great	picture	tie
art	how	place	to
bike	I	pretty	today
boat	is	rope	too
boy	kids	scissors	toy
can	let's	see	use
carve	like	smart	want
do	mice	so	we
draw	my	soap	well
face	nice	some	what
flower	of	start	will
fruit	or	teach	you

About the Author

Bob Reese lives with his wife Nancy in the mountains of Utah with two dogs and five cats. They have two daughters, Natalie who is a resource teacher in Utah and Brittany who is studying to be a dancer in New York City.

Bob worked for Walt Disney and Hanna Barbera studios and has a BA degree in art and business.